# DEXTER'S BIG SWITCH

## BY PAM POLLACK AND MEG BELVISO

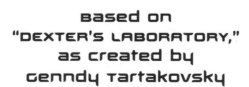

### BASED ON "DEXTER'S LABORATORY," AS CREATED BY GENNDY TARTAKOVSKY

SCHOLASTIC INC.

New York   Toronto   London   Auckland   Sydney
Mexico City   New Delhi   Hong Kong   Buenos Aires

No part of this publication may be reproduced in whole or in part,
or stored in a retrieval system, or transmitted in any form or by any means,
electronic, mechanical, photocopying, recording, or otherwise, without written
permission of the publisher. For information regarding permission,
write to Scholastic Inc., Attention: Permissions Department,
557 Broadway, New York, NY 10012.

ISBN 0-439-44947-2

Cover and interior illustrations by Robert Roper
Designed by Maria Stasavage

12 11 10 9 8 7 6 5 4 3 2 1          3 4 5 6 7 8/0

Printed in the U.S.A.
First printing, October 2003

Just one more turn of the wrench and Dexter, boy genius, would stun the scientific world once more. Using his Virtual Identity Teleporter, Dexter would be able to switch personalities with anyone or anything he wished — even a lab rat.

"You are no longer simply a rodent, my friend," Dexter cooed to the tiny animal

in his hand. "Today you will feel what it is to be Dexter, boy genius. Lucky beast!"

Dexter tightened the last bolt on the Virtual Identity Teleporter. He pointed one end of the Teleporter at the rat and the other at himself. Once he hit the button, his boy genius identity would be scientifically transported into the rodent. He set the timer to transport him back into his own body in two minutes. That would give him enough time to fully experience the inner life of a lab rat. After the rat, Dexter could become a baboon, an elephant, or president of the United States. That would be sure to impress the Young Geniuses of America. Dexter was being inducted into the YGA that very afternoon.

Dexter got into position and reached for the bright purple Identi-mogrifying Switch. "World," he declared, "prepare to meet the first rodent scientist!"

But before Dexter could pull the switch —

"Hi Dexter!" Dexter's sister Dee Dee sang, leaping right in front of the Virtual Identity Teleporter. Dexter jerked his hand away from the switch, lost his balance, and fell over. Dee Dee picked up the rat.

"Ooh! Cute mousie," she cooed.

"Dee Dee, put that down," said Dexter.

"In another moment that lab rat will be smarter than you are."

Dee Dee looked at the rat. Then she noticed the Virtual Identity Teleporter. "Oooooh," said Dee Dee, her big blue eyes turning into saucers. "What's that do?"

"Dee Dee, don't —" Dexter began. But it was too late. Dee Dee had pulled the big purple switch. In an instant, he was transported into his sister's body, and she was transported into his. Dexter and Dee Dee had switched places.

The first thing Dexter noticed was that he was facing the other way. Then he noticed he was holding the lab rat. Then he noticed himself, looking back at him, from the other side of the Teleporter. "Dee

4

Dee," he said, but he didn't sound like himself. His voice was high-pitched and girlie. He cleared his throat. "Dee Dee, you have done a very bad thing."

By now Dee Dee was hopping around in Dexter's body. "Wheeee!" she squealed. Dexter didn't know he could squeal until

he heard Dee Dee squeal with his mouth. "Look at me!" she cried. "I'm Dexter, boy genius ballerina!"

Dee Dee — that is, Dee-Dee-in-Dexter's-body — started pirouetting all over the lab.

"Dee Dee, stop that twirling this instant!" Dexter — that is, Dexter-in-Dee-Dee's-body — yelled. "Twirling is forbidden in a laboratory!"

Dexter took a step forward. That's when he realized Dee Dee's legs were a lot longer than his. It was like walking on stilts. Stilts with big feet. "Whoa whoa whoa!" Dexter exclaimed as he teetered far to the left. He windmilled Dee Dee's spaghetti arms and tilted backward. Then he pitched forward.

"Look out below!" his sister cried from his own body as her brother came crashing down — right onto the Identimogrifying

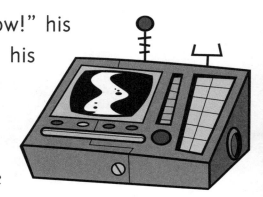

Switch. He landed hard on the floor and looked up at his machine. The switch had broken off completely. Dexter was stuck in Dee Dee's body. Dee Dee was stuck in Dexter's.

"Noooo!" the two siblings cried together.

# Chapter 2

"Waaaaah!" cried Dee Dee. "Stupid science!"

Dexter scowled at Dee Dee. "I am not happy about this either," he said. "And stop that crying. I just got that lab coat cleaned."

Dee Dee cried harder. "How am I supposed to be the Flower Princess in my dance recital today looking like this?"

"What about me?" Dexter said. "Today I am to be inducted into the Young Geniuses of America — the highest honor any scientist between the ages of two and seventeen could wish for. And I'm in the body of a nincompoop!"

Dee Dee marched over to Dexter and stamped on his — her — foot. "Listen up, Mr. Science," she said, scowling up at him.

Dexter wouldn't admit it, but he sort of liked being taller than Dee Dee.

"You turn on your Virtual Whatchamacallit Thing right now and change me back so I can be the Flower Princess!" Dee Dee continued.

Dexter patted Dee Dee on the head. "Believe me, Dee Dee, I want nothing more than to get out of this blonde beanpole of

a body," he said. "But because of your infernal bumbling — which I have warned you about before — we are stuck like this until I can fix the Identimogrifying Switch."

"Fix it now! Fix it now!" yelled Dee Dee, jumping around Dexter's knees. "Fix it —"

"Kids!" Mom called from downstairs. "Time for breakfast — chop chop!"

Dexter and Dee Dee were definitely stuck until after school at least.

They tried to look normal when they came into the kitchen. "Hi princess," Dad said when Dexter walked in.

"Good morning, Daddy," Dexter said, trying to speak like Dee Dee.

"How's it going, champ?" he asked Dee Dee.

"Groovy!" she responded.

"I do not say groovy!" Dexter whispered into Dee Dee's — his — ear.

"You should," said Dee Dee, climbing into the chair where Dexter usually sat.

"I made your favorite omelettes," said Mom, bringing two plates to the table. "Tutti-Frutti Surprise for Dee Dee and Three-Alarm Spicy Man for Dexter!"

Mom put the omelettes down in front of them. When she turned around, they quickly switched plates. "Just keep quiet," Dexter whispered to Dee Dee. "Then they won't notice anything."

Dee Dee nodded. Then she started to talk anyway. "Mom, when we were at the mall, did you see the new miniskirts on sale?" she said. "They're just adorable."

"No, I didn't, hon," said Mom.

Dad was looking strangely at who he thought was Dexter.

"There's one with lace on the bottom that's just soooooo pretty," Dee Dee went on, batting Dexter's eyelashes behind his thick glasses. "I wish I had one!"

Dexter-in-Dee-Dee's-body shook his head violently. But Dad didn't know it was Dexter. Looking confused, he just kept staring at Dee-Dee-in-Dexter's-body. "Dexter, I didn't know you liked miniskirts," he said finally.

"I don't!" said Dexter, forgetting he

was supposed to be Dee Dee. "Skirts are for girls!"

Now Mom was confused. "Yes, dear," she said.

Luckily, the bus came at that moment. Dexter and Dee Dee ran out the door.

On the bus, Dexter didn't know what to do with his big feet. Dee Dee couldn't see over the seat in front of her. And when she

called out, "Hey girlfriend," to her friend Lee Lee, the whole bus stared. "Oops," said Dee Dee, sinking back into the seat.

Dexter kept trying to pull his skirt down over his knees. "It's a little chilly in here, heh heh," he said. When he looked over at Dee Dee she was painting his nails pink with a Magic Marker.

"This is not going to be a good day." Dexter sighed.

# Chapter 9

Dexter bounced down the school hall-way, his pigtails swinging back and forth. Wait. He stopped. *Bouncing?* he thought. *I do not bounce.* But there was something about his sister. . . . Was it the knobby knees? The big feet? The rubbery limbs? Something made him want to bop up and down and skip. "There will be no skipping," Dexter muttered, clutching

Dee Dee's books tight to his — that is, her — chest.

Dexter got to Dee Dee's classroom and stopped. Which one was her desk? He saw her friends Lee Lee and Mee Mee giggling over a magazine. "Hey Dee Dee!" Lee Lee called, waving him over.

Dexter froze for a second. Then he waved and went over to the empty desk beside them. "Hey girlfriend," he said. "Groovy!"

Mee Mee and Lee Lee were looking at the latest *Eleventeen* magazine. There was an article in it about their favorite band, HottieBoyz. "My favorite's Jonathan," said Lee Lee. "He's the shy one."

"I like Zach," said Mee Mee. "He's the

troubled one. Which one's your favorite, Dee Dee?"

Dexter forced himself to look at the magazine and pointed to T.J., the bad boy. He had a killer smile. "This gentleman clearly understands the importance of regular fluoride treatments," he said.

Mee Mee and Lee Lee looked blank. "I mean, he's really cute," Dexter said. He tried to add a girlish squeal like Dee Dee would have. Luckily, at that moment, Mr. Plotzky, Dee Dee's teacher, entered the classroom.

"All right, class, turn to chapter five in your biology textbook," he said. Mr. Plotzky started talking about the life cycle of a frog. Dexter took lots of notes with Dee Dee's glitter pony pen.

Just as Mr. Plotzky got to the exciting moment when the tadpole sprouted frog legs, a piece of purple paper landed on Dexter's desk. He looked around, confused. "Did somebody drop this?" he asked.

Mee Mee and Lee Lee looked at him in shock. Mee Mee shook her head. Lee Lee motioned for him to put the paper away.

But it was too late. Mr. Plotzky had already seen it. "Dee Dee," he said sharply, "what's that in your hand?"

Dexter smirked — ha-ha, it sounded like Dee Dee was in trouble. Then he remembered that he *was* Dee Dee. He brought the paper up to the teacher's desk. Mr. Plotzky unfolded it. It was a drawing of Mr. Plotzky, but instead of regular human legs he had frog legs.

Mr. Plotzky shook his head. "Dee Dee," he said, "you're not paying attention again. What do I have to do to get you to care about science?"

Dexter twitched. His fists clenched. He tried to answer like Dee Dee would have, but he just couldn't. It was too hard. "Science!" he declared. "I love Science! Beautiful Science! Sweet, heavenly Science!"

Mr. Plotzky's eyebrows shot up in surprise. "You love science?" he said. "Well, then, Dee Dee, perhaps you'd like to tell the class how a frog is classified scientifically?"

"Glad to," said Dexter. *"Chordata. Vertebrata. Amphibia. Anura."*

Mr. Plotzky's mouth fell open in surprise. "Could I be this good a teacher?" he whispered.

Dexter went on. "There are approximately 3,500 species of frogs and toads known in the world," he said. "Not counting the three species I created myself. Frogs are the unsung heroes of the amphibian world."

The whole class was silent. Mr. Plotzky looked like he was about to faint.

"And they're really kewl," Dexter added, flipping his pigtails.

Mr. Plotzky was so shook up by Dee Dee knowing the answer to a science question, he gave the kids study hall until lunch. Lee Lee and Mee Mee had forgotten all about it by then. Mee Mee had a new quick-dri rainbow glitter nail polish that

glowed in the dark and smelled like cherries. Dexter had some trouble putting it on, so Lee Lee helped. Dexter stared at his fingers when she was done. He had no idea that nail polish technology had come so far.

But when Mee Mee announced it was time to practice baton twirling, Dexter knew he had to get out of there. He made a break for it, hurrying out of the cafeteria and into the hall. But the person he least wanted to see was coming the other way. It was his archenemy, Mandark — and he was heading straight toward Dexter, er, Dee Dee!

# Chapter 4

Dexter glared at Mandark and clutched Dee Dee's pony pen with the rainbow tail.

Mandark had stopped, too, and he was staring at Dexter strangely. "Ah, we meet again," said Mandark.

"Hello Mandark," said Dexter. The two boy geniuses approached each other slowly. Finally, they faced each other in the middle of the hall.

Suddenly, Mandark dropped to his knees at Dexter's feet. "My love!" cried Mandark. "You light up the school hallway like an exploding star — a supernova!"

It was around this time that Dexter remembered he was Dee Dee today, and that Mandark had a huge crush on his sister.

"Come away, my sweet," said Mandark. "In my laboratory of love we shall discover the chemical formula for romance . . . together!"

"I think I'm going to be sick," muttered Dexter.

"What's that, my love?" said Mandark, popping up off his knees and taking Dexter's hand in his. He pressed the quick-dri rainbow glitter nail polish that glowed in the dark and smelled like cherries against his heart. "Did you speak?"

"Release my hand, sir," said Dexter. "Or suffer the consequences."

Before letting go, Mandark gave Dexter's — that is, Dee Dee's — hand a big kiss. "Consequences be vaporized," he said. Then he spread his arms wide. "A poem, by Mandark," he announced.

"Suffering sulfides," Dexter moaned. "I'm doomed."

Mandark took a deep breath and began. "Pigtails. Swish swish. My heart answers. Thump thump thump. Thump

thump thump thump thump thump. The sky is crying. You are the rainbow of my heart."

*Flaming Freuds,* thought Dexter. *Having Mandark love me is even worse than having him hate me.*

"Thump thump," Mandark finished.

Mandark flung himself to the ground and threw his arms around Dexter's — that is, Dee Dee's — ankles.

"I'm glad I'm not Dee Dee every day," Dexter muttered to himself. "I wonder what kind of horrible day she is having. She has some pretty big pointy boots to fill."

Just then the hallway doors swung open and Dexter's pointy boots walked

right out. Dee Dee —
that is, Dexter — was
surrounded by a crowd
of admirers. "You're the
coolest, Dexter," one of
them said.

"Will you be my
best friend?" asked
another.

"Tell us more about science," said a
third.

Dexter couldn't believe it. Dee Dee was
better at being him than he was! He
started to go over to her, but Mandark
was still clinging to his feet. Dexter
slipped out of Dee Dee's ballet slippers as
Mandark continued kissing them. He

stomped over to Dee Dee and pulled her aside.

"Hi little brother who's now my big sister!" said Dee Dee. "Ooooh! Nice nail polish!"

Dexter noticed that Dee Dee had glued sparkly jewels to his glasses. They'd have to talk about that later.

"Dee Dee," Dexter said. "I hope you have not gotten me into any trouble."

"Trouble?" said Dee Dee. "Not me! You're going to be so happy when you find out what I did!"

Dexter went a little pale. "What did you do, Dee Dee?"

"Well, I was talking to some of your friends from the Young Geniuses Whatchamacallit," said Dee Dee. "And they asked me — I mean YOU — to give a speech at their banquet thingie. And I said yes!"

"But Dee Dee," said Dexter, "the banquet is this afternoon. What if we have not switched back before then?"

"I'll give a great speech," said Dee Dee. "I'll bring my baton!"

## Chapter 5

The rest of the day was sort of a blur. Dexter remembered whispering with Mee Mee and Lee Lee and having no idea what he was whispering about. He remembered playing jacks and getting all the way up to foursies. He remembered learning the difference between goldenberry, boy-senberry, and cherryberry lip gloss.

He remembered acing Dee Dee's math

test, including the extra-credit questions. He remembered Mr. Plotzky crying with joy.

When the school day was finally over, Dexter couldn't wait to get home and fix the Identimogrifying Switch. "I may still have time to practice my speech for the Young Geniuses of America," he said. Just as he got to the school door, Dee Dee — that is, Dexter — stepped in front of him.

"Hold it right there, missy," said Dee Dee, glaring up at him with her hands on her — that is, his — hips. "You're not going home. You have to go to my dance rehearsal because I'm dancing *The Flower Princess*!"

"But Dee Dee," Dexter whined, "I will not have time to fix the Identimogrifying

Switch and become a Young Genius if I am prancing around in a dance class all afternoon."

"Fine," said Dee Dee. "Only if you don't go to my dance rehearsal, I'm going to tell all your Young Genius friends about THIS!"

Dee Dee whipped out an old math test of Dexter's. There was a big A- at the top.

"Oh no!" Dexter cried. He grabbed for the test, but Dee Dee tucked it back into the pocket of her — that is, his — lab coat. "A-," moaned Dex-ter. "Why did I foolishly take a test with my eyes closed? The shame. The horrible shame. Stalking my every

step. The Young Geniuses must never know."

"They won't!" said Dee Dee. "*If* you go to my dance rehearsal."

Half an hour later, Dexter was standing in ballet class in pink tights and a matching leotard and ballet slippers. Next to him was a strong, squat little ballerina with a streak of jagged white in her black hair. "Hello Dee Dee," she said, looking him up and down.

Dexter recognized her as Mandark's scary older sister, Lalavava. Lalavava would be playing Honeybee to Dee Dee's Flower Princess. "Hello Lalavava," said Dexter, looking her right in the eye.

"You may be the Flower Princess now," Lalavava whispered. "But soon I,

33

Lalavava, will rule the flowers. No one outdances me."

Dexter felt his — that is, Dee Dee's — feet twitch. Just being in Dee Dee's body, he knew that nobody could outdance *him* — that is, *her.* When the teacher clapped her hands and started the music, Dexter and Lalavava faced off.

"Behold!" proclaimed Dexter. "The Waltz of the Flowers!"

Dexter began waving his imaginary petals to the music. Behind him six other girls who were playing the Flower Princess's Best Flower Friends swayed, too. "Uh-huh. Uh-huh. Uh-huh," said Dexter. "I'm the Flower Princess. That's right."

Lalavava sprung up on tiptoe. She

raised her arms up like antennae and furiously wiggled her fingers like an angry bee. Behind her, six other Honeybee ballerinas did the same. Moving fast on their toes, they circled the Flower Friends, jabbing at them with their stinger fingers.

Now the Flower Princess was angry. Dexter leapt away from the Honeybees with his long-stemmed Dee Dee legs. His Flower Friends followed. "Leaping levitation!" gasped Dexter. "I'm defying the laws of gravity here!"

Dexter landed heavily on one foot, causing the music to skip. Lalavava and the Honeybees were

coming at him. "Get her!" Lalavava or-
dered her bees, buzzing angrily.

Dexter and the Flower Friends started
to spin faster and faster. As each Honeybee got close, she was batted away by a
propeller-like petal. Finally, only Lalavava was left. "There can be only one,"

she hissed before launching herself at Dexter, the Flower Princess.

Dexter spun so hard he lost his balance and crumpled to the floor. Lalavava ran right over him, somersaulting into the air and landing in the drinking fountain. Dexter wobbled to his feet and curtsied in triumph.

"Brava! Brava!" the teacher exclaimed. "Way to take a risk, Lalavava. And Dee Dee . . ."

Dexter smiled and waited for the great praise he was about to get.

"You don't seem your usual graceful self today. Maybe you should lie down before the recital."

# Chapter 6

Dexter did not lie down. He didn't even bother to change out of his leotard and tights. He rushed straight to the school auditorium where the Young Geniuses of America were having their ceremony. He had to stop Dee Dee from giving a speech for him and ruining his reputation as a scientist forever. He ran into the audito-

rium, scanning the room for himself. But he did not see himself anywhere.

"Where is that Dee Dee?" Dexter muttered. "If she takes the stage I am ruined!"

As if on cue, Dee Dee — that is, Dexter — walked out onto the stage. Actually, she skipped in her little pointy boots. She climbed up behind the podium and looked down at the audience. "How very strange," muttered Dexter to himself. "I see myself on the stage, but I am not there with myself. I feel like a prime number that's just been divided by two with no remainder. I'm mathematically impossible."

On stage, Dee Dee tapped the micro-

phone. "Hello?" she said. "Is this thing on? Hi my fellow genius guys. I'm Dexter. I've written a little essay thingie about what this club means to me."

Dee Dee cleared her throat and adjusted her — that is, Dexter's — glasses. "Science," she began. "Science is really good. What I like about Science is, let's say you're lonely one day. You can build a robot. And he will be your friend. But make sure he's a nice robot. Or he'll smash up your lab."

Dexter shrunk down in his seat. What would the Young Geniuses think of Dee Dee's nonsense?

In front of him, one genius whispered to another. "He makes an interesting point about the isolation of scientific discovery."

His friend nodded. "And the 'not nice robot' obviously symbolizes man's ambition run amok. Dexter is brilliant."

Dexter sat up in his seat. Did these two geniuses just say he — that is, Dee Dee — was brilliant?

Dee Dee went on. "In Science there's always lots of buttons to push and switches to pull. Sometimes it makes people mad when you push the buttons and pull the switches, but if you don't you'll never know what they do. Besides, buttons and switches are fun."

Dexter rolled his eyes. The last switch Dee Dee had pulled had caused her to be onstage babbling nonsense while he sat in the audience wearing pink ballet slippers!

The other scientists buzzed excitedly. "He presents a passionate defense of radical thinking," said one.

"I wonder if he'd let me quote him in the *Astrophysics and Genetic Mutations* newsletter," said another.

Dexter quickly stuck his head in between them. "Sure he would," he said. "I'm Dexter's sister, Dee Dee, and he's been getting that newsletter since he was a baby."

Dexter was so excited at being quoted — well, almost quoted — in the newsletter that he didn't even notice when Dee Dee took out her baton.

"Gimme an S!" she shouted.

"S!" yelled the geniuses.

"Gimme an I! Gimme an E! Gimme an N! Gimme a C! Gimme an E! What does it spell?"

The geniuses hesitated.

"It spells *sience*," Dexter muttered, "which is not a word."

"Einstein misspelled relativity all the time," the genius beside him scolded. "Three cheers for Science, however it's spelled!"

When the three cheers were over, Dee Dee lit her baton on fire and started twirling. The geniuses were transfixed. They had never seen a flaming baton before. (They didn't get out much.)

Dee Dee tossed her baton into the air one last time before Dexter dragged her off the stage. "We have to get home and fix the Virtual Identity Teleporter," he said. "Because I am NOT dancing the Flower Princess at the recital tonight."

# Chapter 7

The front door slammed. Mom looked up and saw Dexter dragging his sister by the hand. "Come on!" said Dexter. "Let's get to work! We don't have much time before the big dance recital! I can't wait! I love flowers! I love ballet!"

"Okay, okay," said Dee Dee. "If you continue pulling me in that violent fashion you are sure to yank my humerus bone

45

completely out of my shoulder socket. Then YOU will never be able to dance the Flower Princess."

Dexter skipped up the stairs. Dee Dee stomped after him. Mom shook her head. "Oh, those two," she said to herself. "Nothing ever changes."

Up in the lab, Dexter picked up his favorite wrench and dropped it. "Stupid Dee Dee hands," he sputtered, bending down to pick it off the floor.

"I don't like being in your body either," said Dee Dee. "Shrimp boat!"

"Flamingo butt!" Dexter shot back.

"You're shaped like a fire hydrant!"

"And you're shaped like a telephone pole with stupid pigtails!"

Dee Dee glared up at him from her fire hydrant body. Dexter scowled down at her from his telephone pole body.

"Gimme that wrench!" Dee Dee shouted, jumping up and grabbing it out of Dexter's hand.

"Dee Dee, get off!" Dexter yelled. Dexter pulled on the wrench as hard as he could. "Give me this wrench right now or I'll . . ."

"Okay," said Dee Dee. She let go of the wrench. Dexter fell back, his — that is, Dee Dee's — long legs flying out from under him. He crashed right into the Virtual Identity Teleporter, leaving a huge dent in its side.

"Waaaa!" wailed Dee Dee. "You broke it more!"

"Kids!" Mom called from downstairs.

47

"Almost ready? It's time for Dee Dee's dance recital."

Mom and Dad were waiting by the door a few minutes later when Dexter and Dee Dee came downstairs. They were carrying what looked like a brilliant scientific invention — only it was covered in ribbons, paper flowers, and jingle bells.

"What's that, kids?" Dad asked.

"This is for the show," said Dexter, still in Dee Dee's body. "It is the Flower Princess's greatest invention. But it is top secret, so you cannot look at it."

"It's neat-o mosquito!" added Dee Dee with Dexter's mouth.

As they carried it to the car Dexter whispered, "Okay, Dee Dee, you will wait

backstage and stay out of my way. I will use my genius to fix the Identimogrifying Switch. Once the switch is fixed we will return to our own bodies. It should take but a moment."

It took longer than a moment. When the curtain went up, Dexter was still in Dee Dee's body.

"That's your cue!" Dee Dee whispered, hearing the music to the Flower Princess theme.

"I am not going out onstage dressed as a Flower Princess with a daisy crown!" Dexter hissed back.

"Oh yes you are!" said Dee Dee. She pushed her body onto the stage in much the same way that Dexter pushed her out of his lab at least once a day.

Dexter stumbled out in front of his Flower Friends. For a long moment he just stared at the audience. He couldn't remember anything he'd learned in rehearsal. So he did the only dance he knew: a polka he'd learned at a family wedding. The Flower Friends polka'd right along with him.

Dexter started adding some high kicks.

He shouted "Hey!" with each one. "Hey! Hey! Hey! Hey!" He kicked his way off-stage and into the wings, where Dee Dee was waiting with the wrench.

"Hurry, hurry!" she squealed.

"I am fixing as fast as I can," Dexter muttered, spinning the wrench. He almost had it when the Flower Friends high-kicked themselves into the wings, picked him up, and carried him back out. They placed him right in the center of the stage. Before Dexter could move, a dark, whirling shape appeared, knocking him over. It was Lalavava, the Honeybee. She was out for blood.

"Feel my stinger," she cackled. Lala-vava began to spin. In moments Dexter was surrounded by Lalavava's Honeybees,

buzzing and backing up straight at him with their stinger behinds.

But Dexter had a secret weapon. He had Dee Dee's steel spring legs. "Geroni-mooooooo!" he cried, leaping straight over Lalavava's head and into the wings.

"Must fix Transporter. Must fix Transporter," he panted, frantically reattach-

ing, realigning, and recali-
brating the Identimogrifying
Switch. "Now all I have to do
is —"

The Honeybees were back.
They grabbed Dexter and shoved
him out on the stage. The music
was getting faster. Lalavava was
chasing the Flower Friends around with
her Magic Stinger and trapping them one
by one in her Honeycomb of Doom.

"We meet again, Flower Princess," she
said, turning to face Dee Dee — that is,
Dexter. Lalavava sped toward him and
leapt up at his petaled daisy crown. Little
did she know that Dexter had made some
scientific adjustments to his Flower
Princess costume.

"Flytrap up," he said calmly, pressing a button under a petal. There was a humming sound as hinged metal leaves with bristles sprouted from his daisy crown. The leaves opened wide. *Schoomp!* The leaves shut tight with Lalavava inside. The Flower Friends cheered. The Honeybees bumped into each other in confusion. The Flower Princess blew kisses to them all and backed slowly off the stage.

Dexter removed the Flytrap attachment from his crown. He could hear Lalavava pounding her fists inside. Dexter ran to the Virtual Identity Teleporter and fired it up. Dee Dee hopped up and down impatiently as he pointed the ray at her. Dexter stood on the other side, hand poised over the Identimogrifying Switch. On stage,

the Flower Princess's solo was about to begin. "Dee Dee," he said, "I hope you've learned your lesson about . . ."

Dee Dee reached out and gave the Identimogrifying Switch a good yank. A split second later, Dexter was watching her, in her own body, in her own Flower Princess costume, as she scampered out into the spotlight.

# Chapter 8

Dee Dee's solo got eight standing ovations. Dexter let Lalavava out of the Daisy Flytrap. The first thing she saw was her brother, Mandark, handing Dee Dee a bouquet of roses.

"You were exquisite, my love," he gushed, dropping to one knee at Dee Dee's feet.

"MAAAAANNNNDAAAARK!!!!" Lalavava bellowed.

Mandark took one look at his furious sister and ran for his life.

"You can't get away from me!" Lalavava shouted, running after him.

"Heh heh heh," said Dexter, watching them go. "Good luck, Mandark."

Mom and Dad were thrilled with the whole show. "You sure showed that Honeybee a thing or two, hon," Dad said, giving Dee Dee a hug.

"You'll always be our princess!" said Mom.

Dad leaned back against the Virtual Identity Teleporter. "I remember my days in the theater," he said. "I was something, wasn't I, hon?"

"You sure were," said Mom, leaning over the Identimogrifying Switch to kiss him.

Dee Dee picked up Dexter and gave him a big squeeze. "I'm glad I'm bigger than you again," she said.

"I am just glad everything is back to normal," said Dexter when she put him down. "Now everyone is who they are supposed to be."

"Time to go, kids," said Dad. "I made daisy cupcakes and princess pudding!"

Dexter and Dee Dee frowned at Dad,

then at each other. Dad never made cupcakes. Mom made cupcakes. Dad ate
them.

"I can't wait, hon," said Mom. "Nobody makes cupcakes like my fine-
lookin' lady!"

"That's my man!" Dad giggled.

Dexter looked with horror at his mixed-up parents.

"Oh, those two," said Dee Dee, throwing an arm around Dexter. "Nothing ever changes."

# THE END

# dexter proudly presents his greatest inventions since the multiple particle acceleration module.

DEXTER'S LABORATORY™

## check out dexter's latest inventions at your local retailer!

**VOLUME INFO:**

PARTY GOODS

INTERACTIVE

APPAREL

FOOTWEAR

BEDDING

CARTOON NETWORK